The Exciting Adventures of Snowball the Brave Chicken

This is a work of fiction. Names, characters, businesses, organizations, places, events, and incidents either are the product of the author's imagination or are used fictitiously. Any resemblance to actual persons, living or dead, events, or locales is entirely coincidental.

The following trademarked terms are mentioned in this book: Mohamed El Afia. The use of these trademarks does not indicate an endorsement of this work by the trademark owners. The trademarks are used in a purely descriptive sense and all trademark rights remain with the trademark owner.

Cover design by el Emma afia.

This book was typeset in Emma afia.

First edition, 2023.

Published by Emma Afia.

Chapter 1: Snowball's Big Idea

- Introduce Snowball, a brave and curious chicken who dreams of adventure
- Snowball convinces her fellow chickens to let her explore the outside world
- Snowball sets off on her adventure, eager to see what lies beyond the coop

Chapter 2: A Dangerous Encounter

- Snowball encounters a wily fox who tries to catch her for dinner
- Using her quick thinking, Snowball manages to outsmart the fox and escape
- Snowball realizes that the outside world is full of dangers, but she refuses to give up on her adventure

Chapter 3: A Helping Hand

- Snowball meets a friendly farmer who offers her shelter and food
- Snowball discovers that not all humans are scary, and she enjoys spending time with the farmer
- However, Snowball knows that she must continue her adventure and sets off again

Chapter 4: Lost and Found

- Snowball gets lost in a dense forest and can't find her way back to the coop
- She encounters a wise old owl who helps her find her way
- Snowball learns the importance of asking for help when she needs it

Chapter 5: The Return Home

- Snowball finally makes it back to the coop, happy to be reunited with her fellow chickens
- She tells them all about her adventure and encourages them to be brave and curious too
- Snowball realizes that sometimes the best adventures are the ones you have with your friends and family.

Chapter 1: Snowball's Big Idea

As Snowball looked out of her cozy coop, she couldn't help but wonder what lay beyond the fence. She had heard stories of the world outside - of lush green fields, towering trees, and babbling brooks. Snowball was a curious chicken and longed to explore the outside world.

One day, she gathered her courage and approached her fellow chickens. "I want to go on an adventure," she said. "I want to see what's out there beyond the coop." Her fellow chickens were hesitant at first, but Snowball's enthusiasm was infectious. Soon, all the chickens were clucking excitedly about Snowball's big idea.

Snowball knew that she couldn't do it alone. She needed the help of her friends to make her adventure a reality. Together, they worked to create a plan. They decided to wait until the farmer was busy with his chores, and then they would sneak out of the coop and explore the world beyond.

The day of the big adventure arrived, and Snowball and her friends eagerly awaited their chance to escape. Finally, the farmer became distracted, and they saw their chance. Snowball led the way as they scrambled out of the coop and into the wide-open world beyond.

Chapter 2: A Dangerous Encounter

As Snowball and her friends made their way across the field, they suddenly heard a rustling in the bushes. Before they knew it, a sly fox appeared, eyes fixed on the chickens. The chickens clucked in fear, but Snowball stood tall and faced the fox head-on.

The fox licked his lips, relishing the thought of a delicious chicken dinner. Snowball knew that she had to act fast. She thought quickly and hatched a plan. "Hey, Mr. Fox!" she crowed. "I bet you can't catch me!"

The fox took the bait and lunged at Snowball. But Snowball was quick, and she darted to the side, narrowly avoiding the fox's grasp. The fox stumbled and fell, giving Snowball and her friends a chance to escape. They ran as fast as they could, hearts pounding in their chests.

After a while, they stopped to catch their breath. Snowball was relieved that they had made it out alive, but she knew that they still had a long way to go on their adventure. She encouraged her friends not to give up, and together they continued on their journey.

Chapter 3: A Helping Hand

As the sun began to set, Snowball and her friends grew tired and hungry. They had been exploring for hours, and their little legs were starting to ache. Just as they were starting to lose hope, they spotted a farmhouse in the distance.

Snowball led the way, and they soon found themselves at the doorstep of a kind farmer. The farmer welcomed them with open arms and gave them a cozy place to rest for the night. Snowball and her friends were grateful for the farmer's kindness and enjoyed the delicious meal that he provided.

As they sat by the warm fire, Snowball and the farmer talked for hours. The farmer shared stories about his own adventures, and Snowball told him all about her big adventure. Snowball was amazed at how much there was to learn about the world beyond the coop.

Eventually, it was time for Snowball and her friends to leave. Snowball thanked the farmer for his hospitality and said goodbye to her new friend. As they left, Snowball couldn't help but feel grateful for the kindness of strangers. She knew that there was still so much more to discover in the world outside the coop.

Chapter 4: Lost and Found

As Snowball and her friends continued on their journey, they came across a dense forest. The trees were tall and the leaves were thick, and they could barely see the path ahead. They were excited to explore this new terrain, but soon they realized they were lost.

The sun had set, and they were stuck in the middle of the forest with no idea how to get back. They huddled together, feeling scared and alone. Just as they were starting to lose hope, they heard a hoot in the distance. It was an old owl, perched on a branch nearby.

Snowball and her friends approached the owl, hoping he could help them find their way back to the coop. The owl was wise and kind and promised to help them. He flew high above the trees, scanning the landscape for any signs of the coop.

After a while, the owl spotted the familiar coop in the distance. He guided Snowball and her friends back to the safety of their home. Snowball was grateful for the owl's help and thanked him for his guidance. She knew that she would never have found her way back without his help.

Snowball realized that even when things seem hopeless, there is always someone willing to help. She knew that she would continue to face challenges on her adventures, but she was excited to face them head-on with the help of her friends and allies.

Chapter 5: The Return Home

After their big adventure, Snowball and her friends returned to the safety of their coop. They were tired, but they felt proud of what they had accomplished. They had explored the world outside, faced danger, and made new friends along the way.

As they settled back into their coop, Snowball couldn't help but feel grateful for the life she had. She had always been content in her little world, but now she realized that there was so much more out there. She promised herself that she would continue to explore and learn about the world beyond the coop.

Over the next few days, Snowball and her friends regaled the other chickens with tales of their adventure. The other chickens listened in awe as Snowball described their encounter with the sly fox and the kindness of the farmer. They were inspired by Snowball's bravery and determination.

As the days passed, Snowball and her friends settled back into their routine, but they knew that they were forever changed by their adventure. They had discovered the beauty of the world beyond the coop, and they knew that they would never be content with the mundane again.

Snowball looked out of the coop and felt a sense of excitement at the thought of all the adventures that lay ahead. She knew that the world was full of wonders and that there was so much more to explore. She knew that she was ready for whatever came next.

The End

Cover design by el Emma afia.

This book was typeset in Emma afia.

First edition, 2023.

Published by Emma Afia.

Made in the USA
Las Vegas, NV
27 October 2023